This book belongs to:

....

I celebrated World Book Day 2021 with this gift fro[m]
my local bookseller and Templar Books #ShareAStor[y]

WORLD BOOK DAY

World Book Day's mission is to offer every child and young person the opportunity
to read and love books by giving you the chance to have a book of your own.

To find out more, and for loads of fun activities and recommendations
to help you keep reading visit worldbookday.com

World Book Day is a charity funded by publishers and booksellers in the UK
and Ireland. World Book Day is also made possible by generous sponsorship
from National Book Tokens and support from authors and illustrators.

Many million years ago,
beyond the path of the lava flow,
on the edge of the jungle, one sunny day,
four little dinosaurs went out to play.

Their mums had told them to keep one eye
peeled for pterosaurs in the sky
and hungry carnivores on the path;
as the others trembled, Bonehead laughed.

GIGANTOSAURUS
doesn't scare me!
I'm too smart to be
his tea!

In fact, I'm a DINO-EXPERT!
I really am the BEST!
You might know the names of some,
but I know ALL the rest.

I've made this thing I call a BOOK.
I might let you three have a look.
We'll play my game called DINO-SPOT.
To win, you'll have to spot the lot!
I found these juicy berries,
bigger than your eyes!
They do look quite delicious
and they will be our PRIZE!

PARA...SAURO...
...LOF...OROS!
That's ONE-nil to me!
It's because I'm VERY clever,
I'm sure you all agree!

"Parasaurolophus," sighed Bill.

"That's my mum, up on the hill."

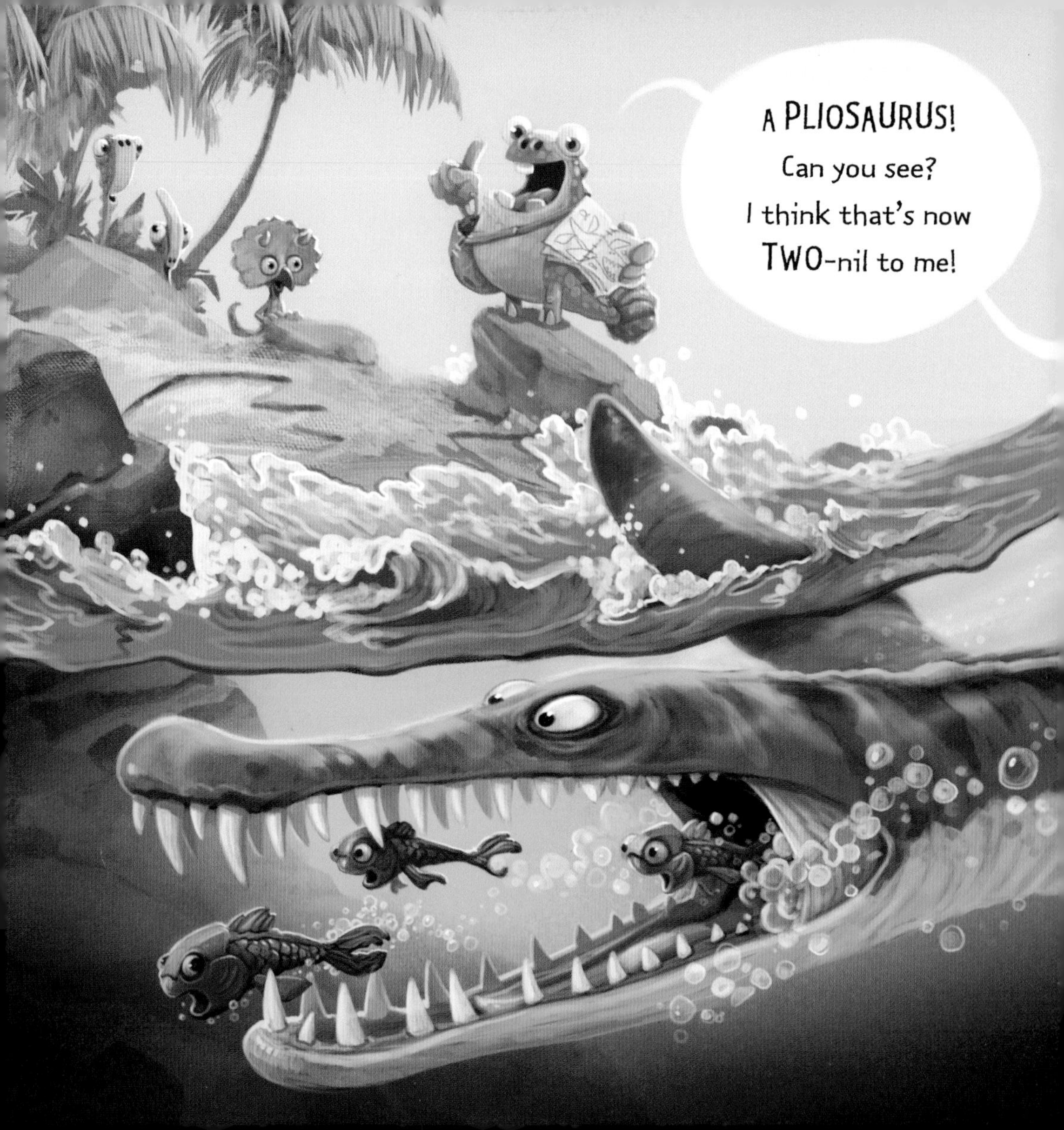
A PLIOSAURUS!
Can you see?
I think that's now
TWO-nil to me!

Gosh, I'm good at spotting!
To win, it's first to three.
I think we'd get a better view
if we climbed that tree.

His friends now knew their hopes were sunk
as Bonehead scurried up the trunk.
From branch to branch to branch he hopped,
then high above them Bonehead stopped.

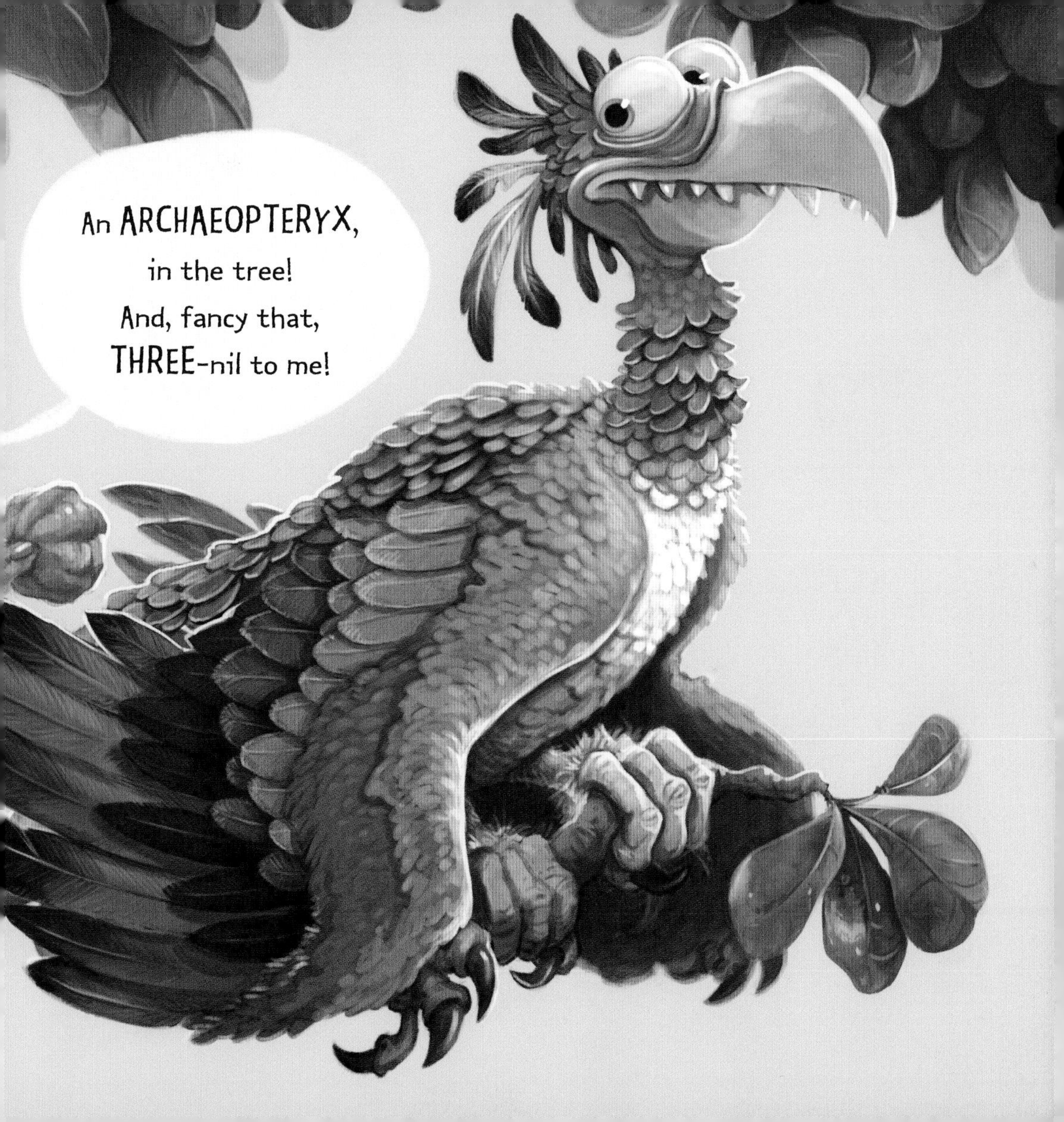
An ARCHAEOPTERYX,
in the tree!
And, fancy that,
THREE-nil to me!

I'm the WINNER! I'm the BEST!
For you three numbskulls I'd suggest: buy a book and use your eyes! Now I'm off to scoff my PRIZE!

Thrilled to be the winner,
Bonehead didn't hear
the creak and crack of falling trees
as something **BIG** drew near.

The others called to warn him,
they whispered, "Run and hide!"
But Bonehead just ignored them,
however hard they tried.

When Bonehead sat to eat his lunch,
the GIGANTOSAURUS' jaws went...

CRUNCH?

Also by JONNY DUDDLE:

Watch the series and read the books: